The
Hoppameleon

For Careoleeine and frog-lovers
shorter than a table

First edition for the United States and Canada published in 2001
by Barron's Educational Series, Inc.

Text and illustration © 2001 Paul Geraghty. Reprinted
by arrangement with Barron's Educational Series, Inc.,
Hauppauge, NY. All rights reserved.

Paul Geraghty has asserted his right under
the Copyright, Designs and Patents Act, 1988,
to be identified as the author and illustrator of this work

First published in the United Kingdom in 2001 by
Hutchinson Children's Books
The Random House Group Limited
20 Vauxhall Bridge Road, London SW1V 2SA

All inquiries should be addressed to:
Barron's Educational Series, Inc.
250 Wireless Boulevard
Hauppauge, NY 11788
http://www.barronseduc.com

Library of Congress Catalog Card Number 00-111611

International Standard Book Number 0-7641-5406-0

Printed in China
9 8 7 6 5 4 3 2

The Hoppameleon

PAUL GERAGHTY

BARRON'S

Long before you were born, when the world was still quite young, there was a sleepy, slurpy swamp. And as the drowsy insects buzzed above the water, a very odd-looking creature swam below.

Then, its beautiful eyes popped up.

The world was filled with color. So out hopped the creature, all green and glossy, and started to chirp, "Calling anyone like me! I'm looking for a friend! Calling anyone like me!"

When something tasty landed nearby, the chirping stopped. Its huge mouth opened, and out shot a long, sticky tongue ...

... which hit another long, sticky tongue.
"Who do you think you are," bellowed the chameleon, "trying to steal my dinner?"
"I—I don't know," said the very odd-looking creature. "I'm just looking for a friend. Who do *you* think I am?"

"Well," the chameleon grumbled, "you catch food with a long, sticky tongue like mine and I'm a chameleon, so you must be some kind of chameleon, too. Now go away. This is *my* patch!"

"Then I'm a chameleon," chirped the very odd-looking creature, "because I can hunt like a chameleon. And I'm just looking for a chameleon friend."

"But you're hopping just like I do," said a grasshopper, "so you must be some kind of grasshopper, too."

"You're right," said the very odd-looking creature. "In that case, I must be a *hoppa*meleon." And with a splash, it dived back into the swamp.

"Gurgle-gurgle, I'm a hoppameleon!" bubbled the very odd-looking creature,
"because I can
       hop like a grasshopper
       and hunt like a chameleon.
And I'm just looking for a hoppameleon friend."

"But you can swim like I do," said a passing turtle,
"so you must be some kind of turtle, too."
"Then I must be a *turtle*hoppameleon!"
sang the very odd-looking creature,
leaping from the water ...

... and splashing a thirsty parrot.

"Hey!" yelled the parrot. "Who do you think you are, splashing my drink all over me?"

"I'm a turtlehoppameleon," sang the very odd-looking creature, "because I can

      swim like a turtle,
      hop like a grasshopper,
      and hunt like a chameleon.

And I'm just looking for a turtlehoppameleon friend."

"But you can chirp like I do," said the parrot, who had stopped drinking, "so you must be some kind of parrot, too."
"Then I must be a *parro*turtlehoppameleon!" announced the very odd-looking creature, skipping off ...

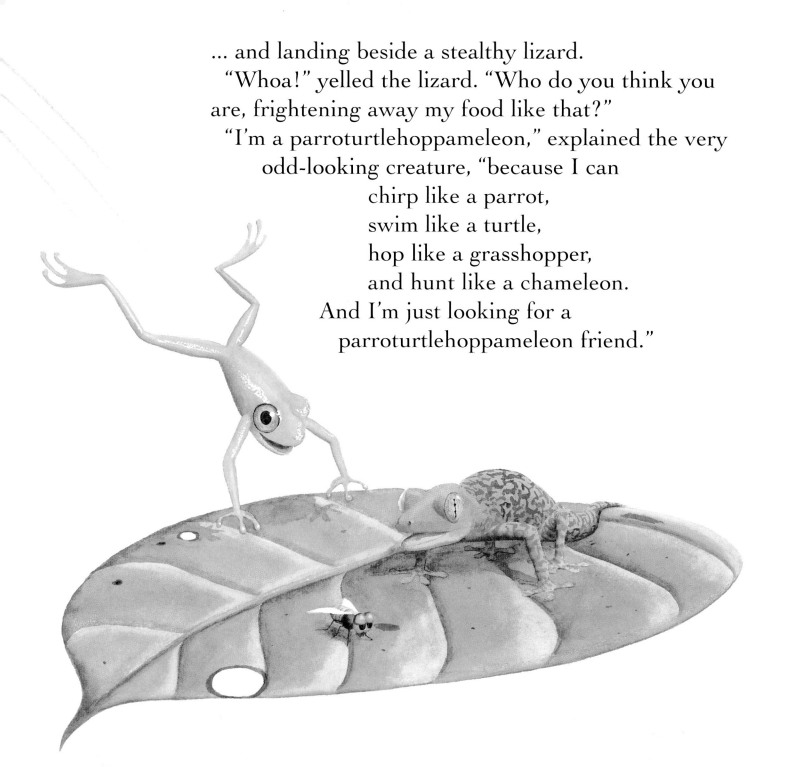

... and landing beside a stealthy lizard.

"Whoa!" yelled the lizard. "Who do you think you are, frightening away my food like that?"

"I'm a parroturtlehoppameleon," explained the very odd-looking creature, "because I can
chirp like a parrot,
swim like a turtle,
hop like a grasshopper,
and hunt like a chameleon.
And I'm just looking for a
parroturtlehoppameleon friend."

"But you cling with padded feet just like mine," said the lizard, "so you must be some kind of lizard, too."

"Well, then I must be a *lizzy*parroturtlehoppameleon," exclaimed the very odd-looking creature,

"because I can
cling like a lizard,
chirp like a parrot,
swim like a turtle,
hop like a grasshopper,
and hunt like a chameleon.
And I'm just looking for a
lizzyparroturtlehoppameleon friend."

"But you have beautiful big eyes like mine," interrupted a bushbaby, "so you must be some kind of bushbaby, too!"

"Then I must surely be a *baby*lizzyparroturtlehoppameleon,"
said the very odd-looking creature, almost out of breath,
"because I can
see like a bushbaby,
cling like a lizard,
chirp like a parrot,
swim like a turtle,
hop like a grasshopper,
and hunt like a chameleon."

"And that must be the longest name in the
whole of the animal kingdom."
    The very odd-looking creature sighed.
"But I would swap all of my names
        for just *one* friend."

Next hop, the very odd-looking creature landed
right in front of another just like itself.
"I'm a babylizzyparroturtlehoppameleon!"
said the very odd-looking creature.
"What are you?"
The other one looked for a moment,
then opened its huge mouth and said ...

"*So am I!* Let's go hopping together!"
 And off they bounced, their rubbery feet making a most peculiar
Frog! Frog! Frog! noise on the lily pads as they went.

Babylizzyparroturtlehoppameleons later got a much shorter name, but I can't for the life of me remember what that name is, or where it came from.
Can you?